Who Said You Can Touch My Hair?

Written By: **Dr. Tamecca S. Rogers**
Co-Author: **London Love & Keith Ross**

Illustrated By:
Brandon Wright

About the Author

Dr. Tamecca Rogers is a Tulsa native author, publisher, columnist, and CEO of a non-profit organization. Through her work, she empowers women and helps teachers and parents approach complex topics and issues with children in a non-threatening manner, such as race, inclusion, identity, and self-love.

Dr. Rogers holds a Bachelor of Arts in Psychology, a Master›s in Business Administration, and a Doctoral degree in Educational Leadership. After serving five years as a hospital corpsman in the United States Navy and a combined six years as a high school instructor and college enrollment counselor, Dr. Rogers held adjunct professor positions at multiple postsecondary institutions before working at Tulsa Technology Center. She currently holds the role of the Director of Diversity, Equity, and Inclusion.

The mother of three children, Dr. Rogers enjoys writing children›s books with her youngest son, Keith Ross. To date, she has published several successful parenting and educational articles, as well as best-selling, award-winning children's books. Her work has been featured on CBS News during an interview with Tanya Rivero and KJRH News during an interview with Julie Chin. To inspire women to act upon their true potential, she co-authored Women Motivated by Purpose and founded Mominate (Mom + Dominate = Mominate), a non-profit organization aimed to help financially challenged mothers and their children.

In addition to boosting children›s self-confidence and motivating women to live up to their highest potential, Dr. Rogers plans to use the profits from her books to assist recovering mothers in Tulsa and help build an elementary school in Mombasa, Kenya.

To learn more about Dr. Rogers please visit www.inspirepublishingllc.com and www.mominate.org.

ISBN: 978-1-7365426-4-4

About the Co-Authors

Keith Ross is a fifth-grader who loves video games, Beyblades, road trips, modeling, and acting. Keith has his own unique style and dances to his own beat. He lives in Tulsa, Oklahoma with his family. In addition to Who Said You Can Touch My Hair? Keith has co-authored Momma May I Be Me?, Now You're It: Journaling to Perseverance, Daddy May I Decide? A Promised Deferred: The Massacre of Wall Street, and Does My Life Matter with his mother, Dr. Rogers. Keith's work has been featured on KJRH News during an interview with Julie Chin. Keith's journey and authorship has been highlighted in the article, Penning Perseverance: Keith Ross, in MetroFamily's Magazine. Keith enjoys reading his books to elementary classes and signing his autograph.

To learn more about Keith Ross, please visit www. inspirepublishingllc.com and www.mominate.org.

London Love is a fourth-grader who loves to roller skate, bike ride and going on road trips. Her favorite destination is Beavers Bend, Oklahoma, where she camps with friends & family. She enjoys a cup of hot chocolate, any time day or night. She's a great cook and enjoys cooking for her family. The most exhilarating experience of her life was going ziplining on a school field trip. London gardens with her mother, Lisa in the summer and enjoys playing with dolls and outside with her younger brother Myles. In addition to co-authoring Who Said You Can Touch My Hair?, London has co-authored Girls Can Be Anything with her cousin Dr. Rogers.

To learn more about London Love, please visit www. inspirepublishingllc.com and www.mominate.org.

Dedication

This book is dedicated to my friend, Lara Skaggs Morris, who inspired me to write this book with my co- authors, Keith Ross and London Love. In 2012, we were in a Technology Center Leadership Administrator program together. By that time, I had already known Lara for eight years. We often talked, laughed, and even cried together.

During a break, she reached out to touch my hair. I reacted by grabbing her hand and saying, “Excuse me, ma’am, what are you doing? You are never supposed to touch a Black woman’s hair!” She looked shocked and said, “Tamecca, your hair is so pretty. I wish my hair could do something like that. I just need to know how it feels.” At that point, all of my grade and middle school moments came rushing back to me. I was teased and made fun of because of my hair. Kids touched my hair for a dare, then ran back to tell their friends how it felt. One boy even attempted to set my hair on fire by throwing a book of lit matches in my coat hood.

Of course, she had no idea what I had been through. These are things we tend to bury and forget about. But unfortunately, the memory is still there. The fact is, getting in anyone’s personal space without their permission is a violation. Lara meant well and is the sweetest, strongest, loving woman I know. So, I have learned we have to give each other grace. I had to educate her about why it was not OK to touch my hair and she respected my wishes. To this day, with her curiosity, Lara still wants to touch, but she knows not to, and I thank her for resisting her urges. Love you, Lara Skaggs Morris! Thanks for being a friend!

Dr. Tamecca S. Rogers

English

My hair is like cotton candy,
And I love how it sits on my head!
And its texture is quite dandy,
All because my mom helps keep it fed.

Kichwa

Nywele zangu ni kama pipi ya pamba,
Na ninapenda jinsi zilivyokaa kichwani mwangu!
Muundo wake ni wa kipekee sana,
Yote ni kwa sababu mama yangu anazitunza vizuri.

François

Mes cheveux sont comme de la barbe à papa,
Et j'aime comment ils reposent sur ma tête!
Et sa texture est tout à fait épatante,
Tout ça parce que ma mère m'aide à les nourrir.

Español

Mi pelo es como un algodón de dulce
¡Y me encanta cómo se sienta en mi cabeza!
Y su textura es bastante dandy,
Todo porque mi madre ayuda a
mantenerlo alimentado.

English

But having beautiful hair like mine
Can get to being quite much,
But that's only sometimes,
When some people want to touch!

Kichwa

Lakini kuwa na nywele nzuri kama zangu
Kunaweza kuwa jambo la ajabu,
Ila ni pindi chache tu,
Pale baadhi ya watu wanapotaka kuzishika!

François

Mais avoir de beaux cheveux comme les miens
Peut devenir un peu trop,
Mais c'est seulement parfois,
Quand certaines personnes veulent les toucher!

Español

Pero tener un pelo tan bonito como el mío
Puede conseguir ser mucha cosa,
Pero eso es sólo a veces,
¡Cuando algunos quieren tocar!

English

I sometimes grunt when they make a demand,
"I must touch your pretty hair," they say.
But it seems they just don't understand!

Kichwa

Nyakati nyingine huwa ninaguna wanapozungumza nami,
Nao husema, "Acha niguse nywele zako zinazovutia".
Lakini inaonekana kwamba hawaelewi!

François

Je grommelle parfois quand ils font une demande,
"Je dois toucher tes jolis cheveux", disent-ils.
Mais il semble qu'ils ne comprennent pas!

Español

A veces hago un gruñido cuando me exigen,
"Debo tocar tu bonito pelo", dicen.
¡Pero parece que no entienden!

English

“Oh, wow!” they say with much fascination,
As they invade my space just to smell!
Some even say it’s been their imagination,
To touch a Black girl’s hair just to tell.

Kichwa

Wanasema hivi kwa mshangao, “Weeee!”
Wanapoingilia uhuru wangu ili tu kuzinusa!
Baadhi yao hata husema wamekuwa wakitamani sana,
Kugusa nywele za msichana Mweusi ili tu waone zilivyo.

François

“Oh, wow!“ disent-ils avec beaucoup de fascination,
Alors qu’ils envahissent mon espace juste pour sentir!
Certains disent même que c’est leur imagination,
De toucher les cheveux des filles Noires juste pour raconter.

Español

“¡Oh, vaya!“, dicen con mucha fascinación,
¡Mientras invaden mi espacio sólo para oler!
Algunos incluso dicen que ha sido su imaginación,
Tocar el pelo de una chica Negra
sólo para contarlo.

English

When I pout, frown, or stump my feet,
They say, "I was just trying to give you a compliment!"
But being seen as someone different is no treat
They're not even trying to be discreet.

Kichwa

Ninapobana midomo yangu, kufura, au kupigapiga miguu yangu,
Wanasema, "Nilikuwa najaribu tu kukusifia!"
Lakini kuonwa kama mtu tofauti si jambo lenye kufurahisha,
Hata hawajaribu kutenda kwa busara.

François

Quand je fais la moue, que je fronce les sourcils, ou que je me cogne les pieds, Ils disent, "J'essayais juste de te faire un compliment!" Mais être vu comme quelqu'un de différent n'est pas un plaisir. Ils n'essaient même pas d'être discrets.

Español

Cuando hago un mohín, frunzo el ceño o doy un pisotón, Me dicen: "¡Sólo intentaba hacerte un cumplido!" Pero ser visto como alguien diferente no es un regalo Ni siquiera intentan ser discretos.

English

Sometimes I wish my hair would grow teeth,
Then people would be scared on their feet.
And maybe even claws would be cool too,
And if they got close my hair would say "BOO!"

Kichwa

Nyakati nyingine mimi hutamani nywele zangu zingeota meno,
Ndiposa watu wangeogopa kunisogezea yao mikono.
Na huenda hata makucha yao yangetulia pia,
Na ikiwa wangenisogelea zaidi nywele zangu
ingewazomea "ILOOOO!"

François

Parfois, j'aimerais que mes cheveux fassent pousser des dents,
Alors les gens auraient peur sur leurs pieds.
Et peut-être même que des griffes seraient cool aussi,
Et s'ils s'approchent, mes cheveux diraient "BOO!"

Español

A veces me gustaría que a mi pelo le crecieran dientes,
Entonces la gente estaría asustada en sus pies.
Y tal vez incluso las garras serían geniales también,
Y si se acercaran, mi pelo diría "¡BOO!"

English

Even though they think it would be flattering,
To try their hardest to touch my hair,
I think that's actually quite shattering,
And I feel this treatment is unfair.

Kichwa

Hata ingawa wanafikiri inafurahisha,
Wanapojaribu kadiri wawezavyo kugusa nywele zangu,
Ninafikiri ni jambo linaloudhi sana,
Na ninahisi kutendewa hivyo si sawa.

François

Même s'ils pensent que ce serait flatteur,
Ils font tout leur possible pour toucher mes cheveux,
Je pense que c'est en fait assez bouleversant,
Et je pense que ce traitement est injuste.

Español

Aunque piensen que sería halagador
que se esforzaran por tocarme el pelo,
Creo que eso es en realidad bastante demoledor,
Y siento que este trato es injusto.

WHY!
WHY!
WHY!
WHY!

English

Why, Why, Why, must you touch it so badly?
They laugh and say it's just so exotic!
So, then I give a big sigh sadly!

Kichwa

Kwa nini, Kwa nini, Kwa nini, mnatamani hivyo kuzigusa?
Wanacheka na kusema ni kitu kigeni sana!
Nami hushusha pumzi kwa nguvu nikiwa nimehuzunika!

François

Pourquoi, Pourquoi, Pourquoi, devez-vous les
toucher si méchamment?
Ils rient et disent que c'est tellement exotique!
Alors, je pousse un gros soupir de tristesse!

Español

¿Por qué, por qué, por qué, tienen que tocarlo tan mal?
¡Se ríen y dicen que es tan exótico!
¡Y entonces doy un gran suspiro
de tristeza!

English

I refuse to be treated like this,
And I wonder why they don't touch each other's.
Instead, they stare and glare
And say, "ours is the norm even though
different colors."

Kichwa

Ninakataa kutendewa kwa njia hii,
Na ninashangaa kwa nini hawagusi nywele za wenzao.
Badala yake, wananishangaa na kunitolea macho
Na kusema, "zetu ni zakawaida ingawa zina rangi mbalimbali."

François

Je refuse d'être traité de la sorte,
Et je me demande pourquoi ils ne se touchent pas les uns les
autres. Au lieu de cela, ils regardent fixement et glissent.
Et disent, "les nôtres sont la norme même s'ils sont de
couleurs différentes."

Español

Me niego a que me traten así,
Y me pregunto por qué no se tocan entre ellos.
En vez de eso, se quedan mirando fijamente
Y dicen: "lo nuestro es lo normal aunque sea de
distinto color."

AHHH!

English

“Ahh!” I yell in frustration!
I might as well pull it all out!
But my hair is God’s great creation.

Kichwa

“Aaahh!” Ninapaaza sauti nikiwa na mkazo!
Ninaweza hata kuzikata zote!
Lakini nywele zangu ni uumbaji bora kabisa wa Mungu.

François

“Ahh!“ Je crie de frustration!
Je pourrais aussi bien tout arracher!
Mais mes cheveux sont la grande création de Dieu.

Español

“¡Ahh!“, grito de frustración.
¡Mejor me lo arranco todo!
Pero mi pelo es una gran creación de Dios.

English

But it's no better at school.
When I walk through the halls
The kids say, "Wow, can I touch... your hair is cool!"

Kichwa

Lakini hali ni hivyo hivyo shuleni.
Ninapotembea kwenye kumbi mbalimbali
Watoto wanasema, "Weeee, ninaweza kugusa nywele zako...
nywele zako ni nzuri!!"

François

Mais ce n'est pas mieux à l'école.
Quand je marche dans les couloirs
Les enfants disent, "Wow, je peux toucher...
tes cheveux sont cool!"

Español

Pero no es mejor en la escuela.
Cuando camino por los pasillos
Los niños dicen: "¡Vaya, puedo tocar...
tu pelo es genial!"

English

I wonder what about my hair is so fascinating.
Could it be the way that it coils?
When they touch my hair, I give a slight smile,
While underneath my skin begins to boil.

Kichwa

Ninajiuliza ni nini kwenye nywele zangu kinachowashangaza.
Je, inawezekana ni kwa sababu zinajisokota?
Wanapogusa nywele zangu, ninatabasamu kidogo,
Huku ndani yangu hasira zinaanza kunipanda.

François

Je me demande pourquoi mes cheveux sont si fascinants.
Est-ce que ça pourrait être la façon dont ils s'enroulent?
Quand ils touchent mes cheveux, je fais un léger sourire,
Alors qu'en dessous, ma peau commence à bouillir.

Español

Me pregunto qué tiene mi pelo de fascinante.
¿Será la forma en que se enrolla?
Cuando me tocan el pelo, esbozo una ligera sonrisa,
Mientras por debajo mi piel empieza a hervir.

English

I hate strangers' hands in my lovely tresses. To be touched without permission really stresses. I want to ask, "Why is my hair so foreign?" "Good grief Lauren!"

Kichwa

Ninachukia watu nisiowajua wanapoweka mikono yao kwenye mistari ya nywele zangu inayovutia. Kuguswa au kushikwa bila ridhaa yako kunachosha. Ninatamani kuuliza, "Kwa nini nywele zangu ni za kigeni hivyo?" "Jamani Lauren!"

François

Je déteste les mains des étrangers dans mes belles tresses. Être touchée sans permission stresse vraiment. J'ai envie de demander, "Pourquoi mes cheveux sont si étrangers?" "Bon sang, Lauren!"

Español

Odio las manos de los extraños en mis preciosas trenzas. Que me toquen sin permiso me estresa mucho. Quiero preguntar: "¿Por qué mi pelo es tan extranjero?". "¡Caramba, Lauren!"

English

Don't confuse this with animosity,
But it's just rude to invade my space just to satisfy your curiosity. It's just weird, Imagine a stranger running their hands through your father's beard.

Kichwa

Usichanganye hili na kutokuwa mwenye urafiki,
Lakini ni ukorofi kuingilia uhuru wangu ili tu kutosheleza udadisi wenu. Inashangaza! Wazia mtu usiyemfahamu akishikashika ndevu za baba yako.

François

Ne confondez pas cela avec de l'animosité,
Mais c'est juste impoli d'envahir mon espace juste pour satisfaire votre curiosité. C'est juste bizarre,
Imaginez un étranger passant ses mains dans la barbe de votre père.

Español

No confundas esto con animosidad, Pero es de mala educación invadir mi espacio sólo para satisfacer tu curiosidad. Es simplemente extraño, Imagina a un extraño pasando sus manos por la barba de tu padre.

English

My hair is magic.
My hair is love.
Given to me from the Father above.

Kichwa

Nywele zangu ni za pekee sana.
Nywele zangu ni upendo.
Niliopewa kutoka kwa Baba yangu aliye juu.

François

Mes cheveux sont magiques.
Mes cheveux sont de l'amour.
Donné à moi par le Père qui est là-haut.

Español

Mi pelo es mágico.
Mi pelo es amor.
Dado a mí desde el Padre de arriba.

English

Only my hands belong on my crown.
And when someone asks to touch my hair.
My reaction is always a huge frown.

Kichwa

Mikono yangu tu ndio inayopaswa kushika nywele zangu.
Na mtu anapotaka kushika nywele zangu
Mara zote hilo hunifanya ninune.

François

Seules mes mains ont leur place sur ma couronne.
Et quand quelqu'un demande à toucher mes cheveux.
Ma réaction est toujours un énorme froncement de sourcils.

Español

Sólo mis manos pertenecen a mi corona.
Y cuando alguien pide tocar mi pelo
Mi reacción es siempre un enorme ceño fruncido.

STOP!!!

English

Touching my hair should be considered a sin.
I don't even know where your hands have been.
Have you even washed your hands today?
Practice social distancing with my hair and just walk away.

Kichwa

Kugusagusa nywele zangu kunapaswa kuonwa kuwa dhambi.
Hata sijui mikono yenu imetoka kushika nini.
Mmeosha mikono yenu leo kweli?
Kaeni mbali na nywele zangu na mwende zenu.

François

Toucher mes cheveux devrait être considéré comme un péché.
Je ne sais même pas où tes mains ont été.
Avez-vous au moins lavé vos mains aujourd'hui?
Pratiquez la distanciation sociale avec mes cheveux et partez.

Español

Tocar mi pelo debería considerarse un pecado.
Ni siquiera sé dónde han estado tus manos.
¿Te has lavado las manos hoy?
Practica el distanciamiento social con
mi pelo y aléjate.

English

My hair is my pride and joy.
My hair is not your toy.
It is something I take very seriously.
And I don't care if you're wondering so curiously.

Kichwa

Nywele zangu ni sababu ya kujisifu kwangu na shangwe yangu.
Nywele zangu si mdoli wenu wa kuchezea.
Ni kitu ninachokichukulia kwa uzito sana.
Na sijali kama mnazishangaa kwa udadisi hivyo.

François

Mes cheveux sont ma fierté et ma joie.
Mes cheveux ne sont pas ton jouet.
C'est quelque chose que je prends très au sérieux.
Et je me fiche que vous vous posiez la question avec curiosité.

Español

Mi pelo es mi orgullo y alegría.
Mi pelo no es tu juguete.
Es algo que me tomo muy en serio.
Y no me importa que te lo preguntes con tanta curiosidad.

English

I know how interesting it must be.
A different style every other day,
As you ask, "How does it stay that way?"
The kinky hair we have is a gift you see.
But I am asking you not to touch it, this I plea.

Kichwa

Najua jinsi ambavyo lazima mnashangaa.
Ninapoweka mtindo tofauti kila siku,
Mnapouliza, "Zinawezqje kukaa hivyo?"
Nywele zetu zinazojisokota ni zawadi mnayoona.
Lakini ninawaomba msiziguseguse, tafadhali nisikilizeni.

François

Je sais combien ça doit être intéressant.
Un style différent tous les deux jours,
Alors que tu te demandes, "Comment ça fait pour rester
comme ça ?" Les cheveux crépus que nous avons sont un
don, tu vois. Mais je te demande de ne pas y
toucher, je t'en supplie.

Español

Sé lo interesante que debe ser. Un estilo diferente
cada dos días, y te preguntas: "¿Cómo se mantiene
así?" El pelo rizado que tenemos es un regalo que ves.
Pero te pido que no lo toques,
esto te lo ruego.

Monday Tuesday Wednesday Thursday Friday saturday sunday

English

Afro puffs on Monday
Braids with beads on Tuesday
Cornrows on Wednesday
Flowy locs on Thursday
Press and curl on Friday
Flat ironed on Saturday
With an updo on Sunday
Please don't touch my hair,
It took a lot of time and a lot of money.

Español

Puffs afro el Lunes
Trenzas con cuentas el Martes
Trenzas africanas el Miércoles
Rastas fluidos el Jueves
Plancha y rizos el Viernes
Planchado el Sábado
Con un peinado recogido el Domingo.
Por favor, no toques mi pelo,
Me costó mucho tiempo y mucho dinero.

Kichwa

Jumatatu ninabana mchicha au afro
Jumanne rasta zilizorembwa
Jumatano mistari iliyopindapinda
Alhamisi mabutu yaliyoachiliwa
Ijumaa mawimbi ya nywele zangu
Jumamosi zinanyooshwa
Jumapili zinabanwa mtindo
Tafadhali msiguse nywele zangu,
Zimechukua muda mwingi kutengenezwa
na pesa nyingi pia

François

Afro puffs le Lundi.
Tresses avec perles le Mardi.
Cornrows le Mercredi
Locs fluides le Jeudi.
Presser et boucler le Vendredi.
Fer plat le Samedi
Avec un updo le Dimanche.
S'il vous plaît, ne touchez pas à mes cheveux,
Ça a pris beaucoup de temps et
beaucoup d'argent.

English

As I switch styles with ease,
Keep your hands to yourself please.
Furthermore, don't ask how much,
And don't touch!

Kichwa

Ninapobadili mitindo kwa urahisi,
Tafadhali zuieni mikono yenu.
Zaidi ya hayo, msiulize ni bei gani,
Na msiziguse!

François

Comme je change de style avec facilité,
Gardez vos mains pour vous, s'il vous plaît.
De plus, ne demandez pas combien,
et ne touchez pas!

Español

Mientras cambio de estilo con facilidad,
Mantén tus manos para ti, por favor.
Además, no preguntes cuánto,
¡Y no toques!

English

Sometimes you may think that it's no big deal,
But you really need to chill.
"Why are you so angry?" You might say.
But I am tired of explaining in a major way.

Kichwa

Nyakati nyingine huenda mkafikiri ni jambo la kawaida,
Lakini kwa kweli mnapaswa kutulia.
Huenda mkauliza, "Kwa nini unakasirika sana?"
Lakini nimechoka kujieleza kwa kina.

François

Parfois vous pouvez penser que ce n'est pas grave,
Mais tu as vraiment besoin de te détendre.
"Pourquoi es-tu si en colère?" Tu pourrais dire.
Mais je suis fatigué d'expliquer de façon majeure.

Español

A veces puedes pensar que no es gran cosa,
Pero realmente necesitas calmarte.
"¿Por qué estás tan enfadado?" Podrías decir.
Pero estoy cansado de dar explicaciones mayores.

English

Would you like it if someone invaded your space?
There is only so much a person can take.
Respect should be equal as we all run this race,
And reach the finish line towards the goals we make.

Kichwa

Je, ungefurahi ikiwa mtu angeingilia uhuru wako?
Kuna mambo machache tu ambayo mtu anaweza kuvumilia.
Heshima inapaswa kupewa kipaumbele tunapokimbia mbio hizi,
Na kufikia mstari wa mwisho kuelekea malengo tuliyojiwekea.

François

Aimeriez-vous que quelqu'un envahisse votre espace?
Il y a des limites à ce qu'une personne peut encaisser.
Le respect devrait être égal alors que nous courons tous cette course, Et atteindre la ligne d'arrivée vers les buts que nous avons fixés.

Español

¿Te gustaría si alguien invadiera tu espacio?
Una persona no puede aguantar mucho.
El respeto debe ser igual mientras todos corremos esta carrera, Y llegar a la meta hacia los objetivos que nos proponemos.

English

When our hair is seen as different or an interest to you
This makes it hard to get along, which is all we want to do.
If you like it just say something nice, use your thinker,
And not your sticky finger.

Kichwa

Nywele zetu zinapoonekana kana kwamba ni
tofauti machoni penu
Hilo hufanya iwe vigumu kuishi kwa upatano,
na ndilo jambo ambalo sote tunatamani.
Ikiwa umezipenda sema tu jambo fulani zuri,
tumia akili zako, Na si mikono yako.

François

Lorsque nos cheveux sont considérés comme différents ou intéressants pour vous.
Cela rend difficile de s'entendre, ce qui est tout ce que nous voulons faire. Si tu aimes ça, dis quelque chose de gentil, utilise ton cerveau, Et pas ton doigt collant.

Español

Cuando nuestro cabello es visto como diferente o
un interés para ti Esto hace que sea difícil llevarse
bien, que es todo lo que queremos hacer.
Si te gusta solo di algo bonito, usa tu pensador
Y no tu dedo pegajoso.

English

So, there's really no need to have to touch.
Because touching my hair is quite a bit much.
We can all be friends and just compliment.
That will prevent the wrong message being sent.

Kichwa

Kwa hiyo ukweli ni kwamba haina haja ya kuzigusa,
Kwa sababu kugusagusa nywele zangu si jambo dogo.
Sote tunaweza kuwa marafiki na kusifiana.
Hilo litazuia tusielewane vibaya.

François

Donc, il n'y a vraiment pas besoin de toucher.
Parce que toucher mes cheveux, c'est un peu trop.
Nous pouvons tous être amis et juste faire des compliments.
Cela évitera d'envoyer le mauvais message.

Español

Así que, realmente no hay necesidad de tener que tocar.
Porque tocar el pelo es un poco demasiado.
Podemos ser amigos y simplemente hacer un cumplido.
Eso evitará que se envíe el mensaje equivocado.

English

A start for how to not offend me,
Is to put yourself in my shoes,
That would help make things quite just,
And in this way, nobody will lose.

Kichwa

Jambo la kufanya ili usinikwaze,
Ni kujiweka katika hali yangu.
Hilo litasaidia kuweka mambo sawasawa,
Na kwa njia hiyo, sote tutafaidika.

François

Un début pour savoir comment ne pas m'offenser,
C'est de vous mettre à ma place,
Cela aiderait à rendre les choses plus justes,
Et de cette façon, personne ne sera perdant.

Español

Un comienzo para no ofenderme
Es ponerse en mi lugar,
Eso ayudaría a hacer las cosas justas,
Y de esta manera, nadie perderá.

English

If you look at my hair and like what you see,
Look with your eyes and not your hands,
And let it be.

Kichwa

Ikiwa unapoangalia nywele zangu unapendezwa
na kile unachokiona,
Zitazame kwa macho yako na usitumie mikono yako,
Na acha iwe hivyo.

François

Si vous regardez mes cheveux et aimez ce que vous voyez,
Regarde avec tes yeux et non avec tes mains,
Et laisse faire.

Español

Si miras mi pelo y te gusta lo que ves
Mira con tus ojos y no con tus manos,
Y déjalo estar.

English

You may be attempting to increase
your cultural understanding.
But touching my hair is pretty demanding.
Don't presume
My hair is your classroom.

Kichwa

Huenda unqjaribu kuelewa zaidi utamaduni mbalimbali.
Lakini kugusa nywele zangu si jambo linalofurahisha.
Usikate kauli haraka
Kwamba nywele zangu ni darasa lako la kujifunzia.

François

Vous essayez peut-être d'accroître votre compréhension
culturelle.
Mais toucher mes cheveux est assez exigeant.
Ne présumez pas
que mes cheveux sont votre salle de classe.

Español

Puede que intentes aumentar tu comprensión cultural.
Pero tocar mi pelo es bastante exigente.
No presumas
Mi pelo es tu aula.

English

The last thing to do, is to teach your kids,
That these ideas of touching others' hair you should rid.
Then they won't grow up making the same mistake,
Because when we are treated differently that's a
feeling we really hate.

Kichwa

Jambo la mwisho la kufanya, ni kuwafundisha watoto wako,
Kwamba wanapaswa kuepuka kugusa nywele za wengine,
Na hivyo hawatakua wakifanya kosa lilelile,
Kwa sababu tunapotendewa kama watu tofauti, hilo ndilo jambo tunalochukia kabisa.

François

La dernière chose à faire, est d'apprendre à vos enfants,
Que vous devez vous débarrasser de ces idées de toucher les cheveux des autres.
Ainsi ils ne grandiront pas en faisant la même erreur,
Parce que lorsque nous sommes traités différemment, c'est un sentiment que nous détestons vraiment.

Español

Lo último que hay que hacer, es enseñar a tus hijos
Que estas ideas de tocar el pelo de los demás debes librarte.
Así no crecerán cometiendo el mismo error,
Porque cuando nos tratan de forma diferente es un sentimiento que realmente odiamos.

English

We hope after reading this you can understand.
It's not fun when you touch my hair with your hand.
When it comes to my hair I don't play.
So, keep your hands in your pockets and have a nice day.

Kichwa

Si jambo linalofurahisha unapogusa nywele zangu kwa mikono yako. Inapohusu nywele zangu, si jambo la mchezo-mchezo. Kwa hiyo, weka mikono yako kwenye mifuko yako, na uwe na siku njema.

François

Nous espérons qu'après avoir lu ceci, tu peux comprendre. Ce n'est pas drôle quand tu touches mes cheveux avec ta main. Quand il s'agit de mes cheveux, je ne joue pas. Alors, gardez vos mains dans vos poches et passez une bonne journée.

Español

Esperamos que después de leer esto puedas entenderlo.
No es divertido que me toquen el pelo con la mano.
Cuando se trata de mi pelo no juego.
Así que mantén las manos en los bolsillos y que tengas un buen día.

www.ingramcontent.com/pod-product-compliance
Lightning Source LLC
Chambersburg PA
CBHW041929010726
47507CB00003BA/230